"What's Dead Mean"?

Doris Zagdanski

Illustrated by Ben Spencer

HILL OF CONTENT

Melbourne, Australia

First published in Australia 2001
by Hill of Content Publishing Pty Ltd
86 Bourke Street, Melbourne 3000
Tel: (03) 9662 2282
fax: (03) 9662 2527
Email: hocpub@collinsbooks.com.au
Website: hillofcontent.bizland.com

© Copyright: Doris Zagdanski 2001

Designed by Ben Spencer
Printed by Brown Prior & Anderson Melbourne

National Library of Australia cataloguing-in-publication data

Zagdanski, Doris, 1954-.
 What's dead mean?

ISBN 0 85572 316 5

1.Death — Psychological aspects — juvenile literature. 2.
Bereavement — Psychological aspects — Juvenile literature.
I. Title.

155.937083

Dedication

For Alana

About Children, Death & Grief

"Often mothers and fathers feel that if only they can answer their children's questions in the 'right' way, or say and do the 'right' things, then their children will not suffer. Yet parents also know there are no satisfactory answers to their own questions, no instant cure for their own grief – and that the same is true for their children." [1]

Children as young as two or three years of age can sense the impact of a death in the family, often signalled by changes in household routines or the appearance of lots of people in their home. Naturally, they are too young to know the real meaning of death, but they are not too young to feel frightened, curious or insecure about the unusual comings and goings around them. Whilst children may not grieve like adults do, they will react to signs of stress around them. A major task for adults is to help children to feel safe amidst all this. [2]

Around the ages of four and five, it will be even more difficult to convince children that all is well because they will overhear conversations, and their eyes will tell them that people look strained, upset or are not behaving in their usual way. Rather than believe that such young children will not be affected by a death, this book aims to help adults understand the needs of children so that they do not become overlooked.

Studies of children's understanding of death have been published since the 1940's. In recent years, many research papers share similar findings:

• Parents generally underestimate the need to inform children, and their motivation to protect their children from hurt means they often refrain from giving children explanations about what has happened;

• Children need to share in family grief—if adults can name their feelings, "I'm sad because Daddy has died", it can be helpful to children who are trying to understand their own emotions;

• The opportunity to participate in farewells is an important learning and healing experience—children sometimes report anger, disappointment and frustration at not being included in these events;

• Given the opportunity and a safe environment, many children are keen to talk about issues surrounding death, they can be endlessly curious and their grief may involve asking many questions—simple, factual answers are the best response rather than a sweeping reassurance that "everything is fine", which may not match what the child is observing;

• The kindergarten and school systems can provide further means for helping children—staff need to be trained to respond effectively to children and have resources available—books, music, art, play activities and written information for parents;

• Children remember many details of a death event for many years, even from the young age of three or four, and they report thinking, dreaming and worrying about it often; they may find they need to re-visit the event through more discussion at later stages in their lives;

• Children often believe their parents have a special ability to "get over" the event—they can become confused by seeing them return to their normal routines at home and work when the child still feels hurt and sad.

When a child's need for involvement and information is not met, often they rely on their imagination to fill in the missing details. This is rarely helpful or accurate, as their version of what happens when someone dies might come from previous learnings based on what they've seen on television, video games or even fairy tales—in these cases death is often the result of some sinister event or violence, and characters often emerge from 'death' ready to face another adventure. So the question for adults is probably not, "Is my child too young to be told about death?", but rather, "How can I tell my child about death in a way that is going to be helpful and match their level of understanding?"

Research shows that children are observant and easily pick up that adults prefer them not to know, talk about or react to the events so they readily conform to adults' wishes—parents especially need to know that the best support they can give their children is to "help them bear both facts and feelings"[3] —
rather than ignore, shield or try to protect them.

III

How To Use This Book

This activity book is intended for children between the ages of 3–7 years and adults of all ages. It is designed to encourage communication between adults and children about the subject of death. It especially helps adults explain the words that children hear when someone they know has died. Research shows that a child's understanding of death can be more advanced than is usually expected for their age and developmental level when they personally experience a loss or death in the family. The "degree of communication and sharing within the family" will also affect their reactions and the way they express themselves.[4]

What makes this book unique is that it aims to teach adults and children about death simultaneously. The left hand pages are like an information guide for adults, especially parents, who will learn about coffins, cremation, grief and perhaps many things they have never been told about death either. The right hand pages contain the child's story line, with explanations that are simple and factual and allow for adults to add more information. Then there is room for drawing, writing, pasting pictures, adding photos—whatever appeals. Both the adult and child can work together—both can talk, write, and draw as they go along. There is plenty of blank space to do this.

As you finish reading each page, you can simply ask, "What would you like to draw here?" Children are likely to want to draw what they want to draw—and it may have nothing to do with death. That's alright, just let them be spontaneous.

Or you can guide their drawings if you wish. For example, when talking about a coffin you could draw the outline of the shape and ask the child to colour it in. If you're explaining about the funeral you could draw the faces of people who attended. If you're describing the cemetery you could help the child to draw a simple version of a headstone or they could press some flowers and later paste them on the page.

You might decide together to create a photo story instead. Favourite photos could be pasted on each page with a few written words explaining why these pictures are special.

The border illustrations can also be coloured in, or the child might like to draw their own version of a dog, some clouds or the house they live in—inspired by what they see around the border. And ask them to keep their eye out for the drawing of the child who "walks along" the bottom of each page.

Whatever you do, it's important not to force their feelings or make their responses artificial. The objective is to spend time together, getting the dialogue started and teaching children that it is alright to ask questions about death. They will also learn that they have not been forgotten—something that is easy for adults to do because of the perception that small children are too young to understand and they will 'bounce back' quickly when someone in their family has died.

Don't be surprised if young children need to be told the same information over and over. You might think they have grasped the idea that death is forever and then the next day they might ask if they can visit the person who has died. They have little understanding of the concept of time—a *long* time for a child can be a matter of minutes, so 'forever' can be a very abstract idea. Be patient and be prepared to repeat information and answer the same questions over and over. Their understanding will increase as they mature.

What makes this book special is that it will become a record—not only of the child's learnings, memories, thoughts and feelings—but of the principles of helping children to understand death—principles which they can pass on to their own children.

"One of the best ways to communicate with children [about death] is to play with them, to sit with them, watch their play and join in at some point... reading books is another form of play that children enjoy and is often a part of everyday family interaction... it is also possible to create a book which is unique to the situation of the child's circumstances and can be developed from his or her own viewpoint... such books are very personal and are treasured by children as they grow older because they usually contain pictures of themselves at the time and can be re-read and examined during future life stages." [5]

This page sets the scene for the the theme of the book—there are some words we know, and there are some we don't. This page allows the child to draw pictures of something they know and begin their involvement in the learning process.

The text purposely begins with some easy words to understand—*hot, cold, red, blue, big, small*—and so you can start by drawing anything which the child associates with these familiar words—hot sun, cold icecream, red dress, blue shoes, big house, small ant.

The experience of a death in the family, or any other significant loss, threatens a child's view of the world. It's not safe. Things aren't predictable, familiar. People aren't behaving like they used to.

Adults need to act in ways that help children to feel safe. Cuddles. Hugs. Not leaving them alone with unfamiliar people. Allowing them to ask questions. Telling them the truth. Not calling their fears silly. Letting them sleep with the light on. All of these communicate that someone is looking out for them. So does talking to them and making the time to give them your attention—like working through the pages of this book together.

Some words are easy to understand.
Hot, Cold, Red, Blue, Big, Small.

Despite what adults may believe, the words *dead* and *die* are familiar to most young children. They have already heard various versions of these words around the home—"dead tired", "dead easy", "scared to death", "drop dead"... the list is endless. They probably won't have associated them with people dying—they know flowers die, a pet may die, and dead birds and insects can be found in the garden. They will also not yet understand that death is permanent. So they often ask if the person is coming back or if they can go to see them. These questions are expected for this age group.

The best way to approach such questions is simply to repeat the information: *"No, Grandma can't come back because she is dead." "No, we can't see Daddy because he is dead, but we can look at his photos and see him that way."*

Some words are not so easy to understand.
Like the word dead. And the word die.
Plants die.
Birds die.
Animals die.
And people die too.

It's important for children to know that dead is *not* like sleeping. It's about life ending—the normal things your body does when you're alive can't be done anymore. One especially important point for the child to know is that dead people don't feel anything—this is often an issue for them when it comes time to being buried or cremated.

It is tempting to use words like 'gone' or 'asleep' when we actually mean 'dead'. These words may actually confuse children because they associate them with their real meanings—their life experience tells them that you can always come back if you've 'gone' somewhere and you will always wake up if you're asleep. This makes sense using a child's logic.

Sometimes adults use the word 'heaven' to explain that someone has died: *"Grandpa has gone to heaven." "God has taken him to be with the angels in heaven."*

Whilst it's alright to refer to your religious beliefs when someone has died, it may create more questions which you will need to answer. The concept of heaven is very abstract. To a young child it's a place, just like any other that you go to. Therefore you can probably come home again or people can visit you there. So they may ask if they can go to heaven to see the person or exclaim angrily, *"I don't like God for taking my Grandpa away. I want him to be here with me."* Be prepared for these kinds of responses. Children are not illogical, their understanding is just limited by their experience.

Another common way adults explain death to children is to say that the person is now a star in the sky. It's best to avoid these statements. Not only are they fictitious, but on cloudy nights or even during the day, children are left wondering where they are now—the special star is gone—and adults will need to create more explanations.

When people die, everything in their body stops.
They stop breathing.
Their heart stops beating and their skin goes cold.
They cannot walk or talk or see or feel anything anymore.
Their body lies very still.
Everything has stopped.
They are not alive anymore.
That's what dead means.

There are two lessons to learn here. Firstly, to ask the question WHY? is an important part of a child's learning process about any subject—so death won't be any different. *Why didn't the doctor make him better? Why did the car crash? Why did she get sick?* The WHY question is often combined with HOW questions. *How did the cancer get in her body? How did he die? How did he get inside the coffin?*

Secondly, the repeated use of the word 'very' is intended to help children distinguish between minor and major events. For example, if you say you're feeling sick usually it passes or the doctor can help you get better. But *very, very, very* sick stresses that this event is far worse.

It's important to reassure children that most people don't die when they get sick and that most people die at an old, old age—but be aware that 'old' will probably be anyone who's not a child like them.

It's hard to understand why people die.
Most of the time people die because they
are very, very old.
Or they are very, very sick.
Or there was a very, very bad accident.
And sometimes we don't know why they die.
Maybe you don't understand everything
about dying yet, but when you're bigger
you'll understand more.

Adults may believe they need to shield children from the reactions of grief like sadness and crying. Children, like adults, need to know it's alright to cry. If you are asked why you are crying, tell the child it's because you're sad and you miss the person who has died. Assure them that even though you are crying you are going to be alright.

It is unhelpful for children to be told that they should be brave or that big boys don't cry—we need to teach children that emotions are a normal part of loss, for boys and girls, for big kids and little kids.

It would also be appropriate to let a child know that sometimes we can be angry or scared or lonely or confused because we don't like what's happened and we wish we could make the person come back. All of these are normal grief reactions and children need to know that it's safe to tell you that they're not happy about what's happening.

Also, be aware that children's grief is often not expressed in words, but through their actions instead. You can expect angry outbursts, regressive behaviour like thumb-sucking, bed wetting, clinginess, fear of you being out of their sight or wanting your constant attention. They may develop a fear of the dark or sleeping problems. Children might also 'act out' what has happened—play dead games and re-enact hospital or ambulance or funeral scenes through their play. Don't worry, this is their way of taking in information and trying to absorb it and make sense of it.

Your role is to give them plenty of hugs and reassurance that you (or someone else they know and trust) will be there to look after them and help them to feel safe.

Sometimes we don't want to believe that people can die. We miss them and we want them to come back. We just don't like it.

It's sad when someone dies because we cannot be with them anymore. When you are sad it's alright to cry.

Children will be curious about what happens to a dead body. Here the responses are factual, and descriptive words are used to help them 'picture' what a coffin looks like.

These days, coffins may be painted in any colour or come in traditional wooden finishes. It is the shape which distinguishes a coffin from a casket—a coffin is wider at the shoulders and then becomes narrow towards the feet, whilst a casket is rectangular in shape and may be made of timber or metal like steel, bronze or copper.

A child might first see the coffin at the 'viewing'— seeing the body helps children (and adults) to understand that life has ended and that there is no pain, no movement, no breathing. This will reinforce the explanations you gave about death earlier. The viewing can be a very valuable, personal time to say goodbye—seeing the person at peace gives many people a sense of relief whilst it also provides a time of 'closure', a time to say the things that need to be said.

Adults need to help prepare children who will attend the 'viewing'. Children need to know where they will be going, who will be there, how the body will look—the body will be clothed, it will be cold to touch, it will be in a coffin, the body cannot move or see or speak or feel anything. They also need to be aware that some people including you and them might cry—saying goodbye is very sad. Children can also be encouraged to write or draw a goodbye letter or picture, or place something special in the coffin.

It's also a good idea afterwards to ask about the experience. *Do they want to ask any questions? Is there something they don't understand? Do they want to tell you anything?*

When people die, their body is put in a coffin. This looks like a long, wooden box which is only for dead people. It's soft inside and has a lid. It keeps the dead body safe.

This page does not talk about the funeral ceremony itself, or give any religious messages—this is best left to you to explain according to what is relevant to your beliefs, experiences and the child's questions and ability to understand. Remember, their questions are the best guide to what they want to know.

Again, there is no mention that the funeral will take place in a church, because it may be at a chapel or even at the graveside only.

Do talk about church and prayers and hymns if it is part of your family's experience.

The easiest way for children to understand about funerals is to actually attend. Beforehand though, they need to be prepared with explanations—where it will be held, who will be there, what kind of things will happen, why people are sad. Children may worry about seeing their family members upset and will need to know that even if they are crying they can still manage.

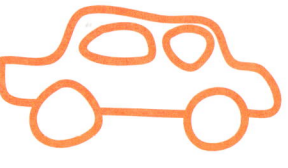

Then we have a special time to say goodbye. It's called a funeral. Lots of people come. They say good things about the dead person. Sometimes they bring flowers. Sometimes they cry because it's sad to say goodbye.

The words 'cemetery' and 'crematorium' will probably be unfamiliar to young children, but remember that at this age they are learning new things every day. They may be difficult concepts to grasp for a young child. They need to know that we don't 'keep' dead bodies—they are laid to rest in a variety of ways. If they have ever experienced burying a dead pet this can be a useful analogy to use. This kind of information may be all they need to know.

Remember also, that even when a child asks where a dead body is, they may not want all the details—they may just want to know if the person is still in the hospital, or their sick bed or the place where they died.

If asked to explain burial in a grave use simple, factual words: a deep hole is dug, the coffin is lowered in gently, earth is put on top and then the grass grows back over it. The coffin keeps the body safe.

Describing cremation is more difficult. It's hard for children to understand why we burn dead bodies. But, in Australia, more than 60% of all funerals are cremation services. One of the difficulties is that children are warned by their parents from the moment they can walk to stay away from hot things—the stove, an iron, a heater, a fireplace. It therefore seems confusing and frightening to burn a person's body, especially because children automatically think you can feel it (that's why we need to explain that dead people don't feel anything anymore). Don't be surprised that even with your best efforts, children will not like the idea of cremation, just as many adults don't either.

Very simply explained, the cremation process usually takes about one hour. Each coffin is cremated separately—that's a guarantee. What we call "the ashes" are the remains of the thickest bones like the pelvis and thigh bones. These are cooled, separated from any coffin debris like nails, and are processed into tiny fragments which are greyish white in colour. These are then packaged, labelled and are ready to be placed in a memorial location.

After the funeral, the coffin goes to a cemetery or a crematorium. There are gardens here where dead people are buried and they have a special sign with their name on it. We can take some flowers there too. But we can't see them anymore like we used to.

One of the most important lessons children can learn about death is that it's alright to talk about the person who has died, even if it makes you sad. This reinforces the idea that death is not a taboo subject. Keeping the lines of communication open—talking about what's happened, continuing to mention the person, talking about how you feel (or writing or drawing)—are viewed as positive ways of dealing with loss and grief—for adults and children.

On this page, children can be encouraged to draw the person who has died or stick on some photos. They can write some simple words about the person or that can be the adult's role. This will become a valuable memento for the child when they're older.

Why not ask, "What do you remember most of all?" Or you can talk about the things that you remember.

You could also ask the child if there is anything that belonged to the person who died that they would like to keep. This is an important part of their grief—to be able to have a connection with what they've lost.

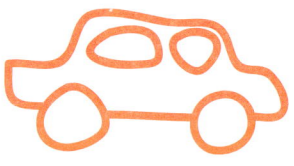

But we can still talk about them.
We can say their name.
We can draw their picture.
Or write a story about them.
We can look at photos.
And we can remember all sorts of things
about them.

This page recognises that there are lots of new or different things that may have been happening because someone significant has died. Even though there has been this opportunity to talk about it by reading this book, some things may still be hard to understand. The message here is that bit by bit, as they get older (bigger) understanding will get easier.

When children have understood what 'dead' really means, they know three truths:
Death is universal—it happens to all living things;
Death is inevitable—all life eventually ends;
Death is irreversible—it is permanent, you can't recover from it.

These facts about death are learned gradually as part of a child's development. During this time, they also need to learn that they can rely on the people around them to help them to feel safe and secure when the predictability of their day to day life has been interrupted by death.

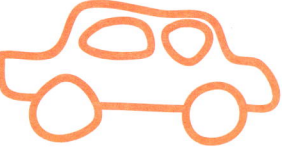

When someone dies there are lots of new things to learn. Maybe you don't understand everything about the word dead yet, but when you're bigger you'll understand more.

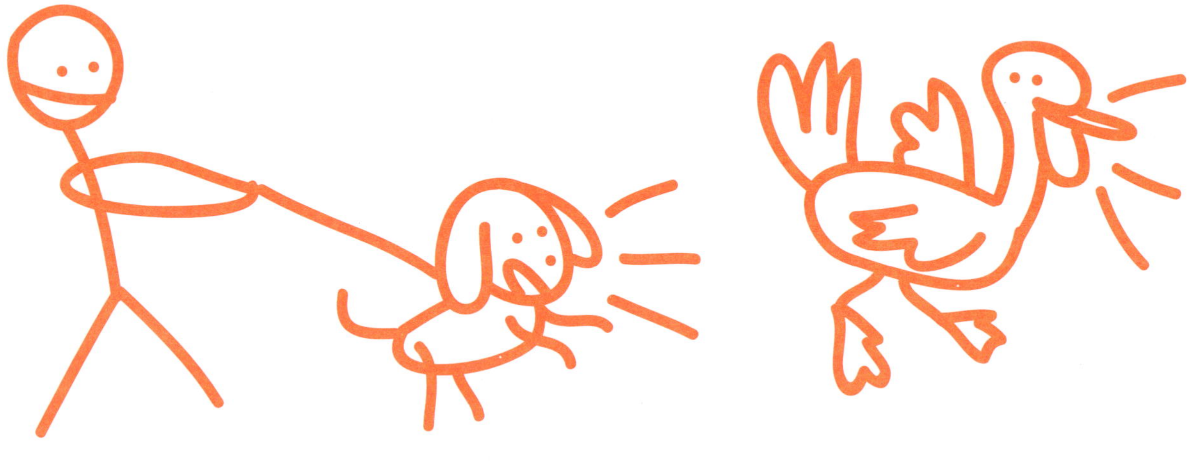